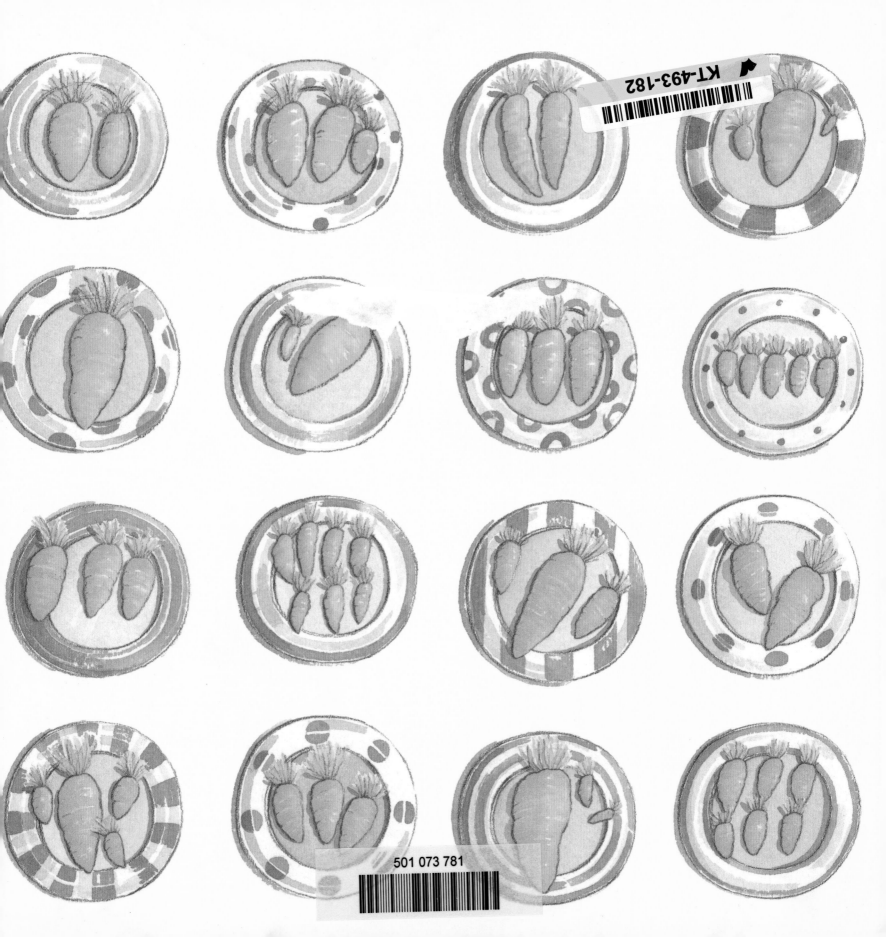

For
Aaron
and Zoë

PUFFIN BOOKS
Published by the Penguin
Group: London, New York,
Australia, Canada, India,
Ireland, New Zealand
and South Africa

Penguin Books Ltd,
Registered Offices:
80 Strand, London
WC2R 0RL, England

www.penguin.com
First published 2006
1
Copyright ©
Penny Ives, 2006

The moral right of the
author/illustrator has
been asserted

Made and printed
in China

ISBN 0-141-38085-3

Rabbit Pie

By PENNY IVES

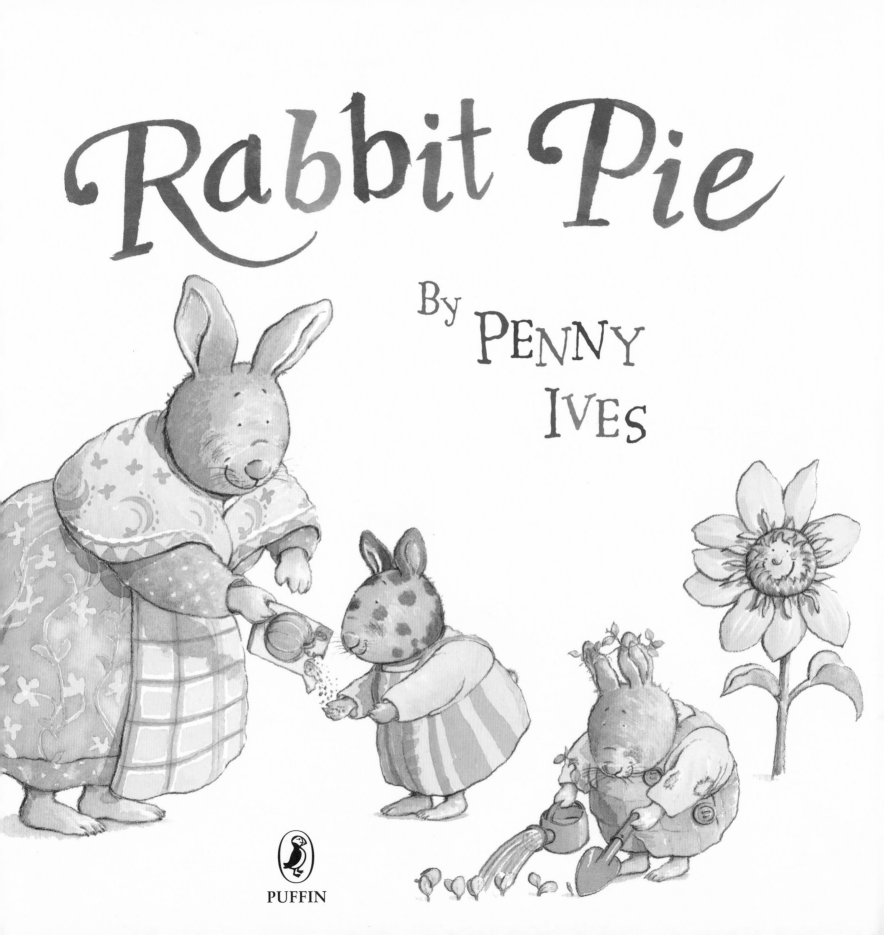

PUFFIN

First gather together
your ingredients.

One game of hide-and-seek
One bath
Six pairs of pyjamas
Six cups of milk
One story
A sprinkling of soft kisses
Six large carrots

Then
find
six
small
rabbits . . .

...if
you
can!

Take off any
dirty
bits . . .

. . . and place in
warm soapy
water.

Gently scrub.

Watch **very** closely.

Fold
into a
soft
towel

and allow to
cool
down.

Pat dry,
dust
the bottoms

and **lightly**
brush
the tops.

Slowly pour in

six
cups
of milk.

Tuck in,
sprinkling
with
kisses.

Leave in a **warm** place
until morning.

When
quite ready,
serve with
fresh
carrots.

Sweet
Rabbit
Pie!

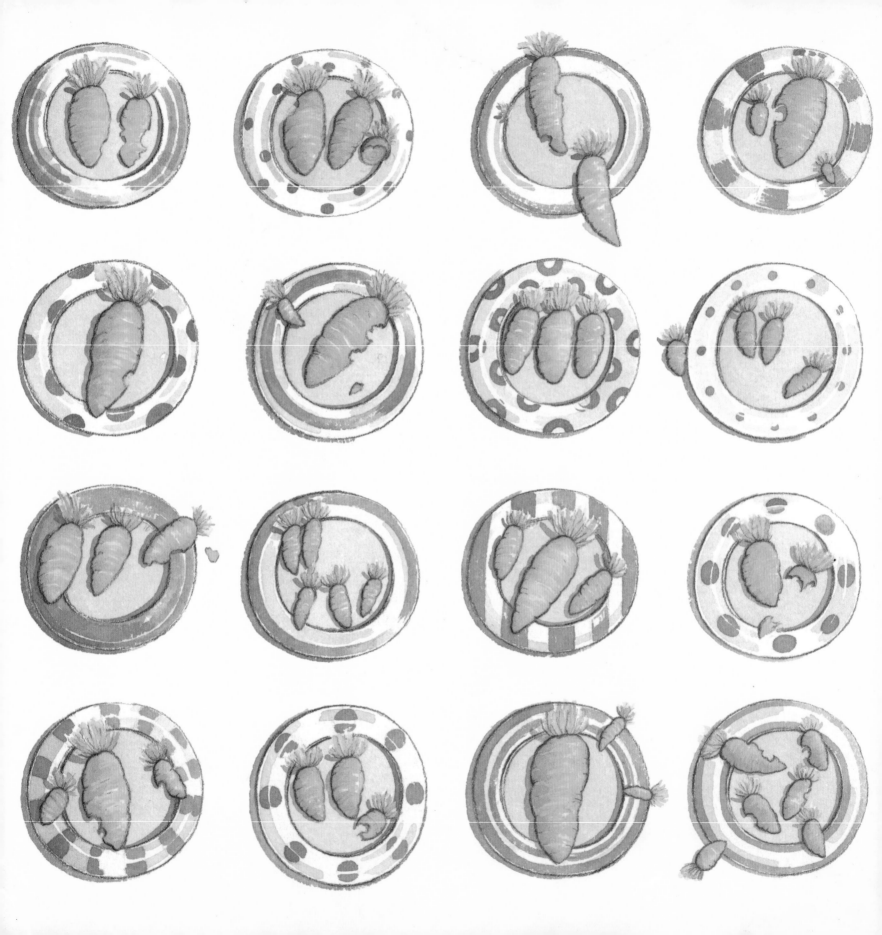